Simon and the wind

Gilles Tibo

Tundra Books

My name is Simon and I love the wind.

When the autumn wind begins to blow
I go out to watch things fly.

I stand on a rock and blow soap bubbles.
The wind carries them off and away.

If I could blow a big enough bubble,
Would it take me flying in the wind?

I run to catch my biggest bubble
But it blows into a tree and breaks.

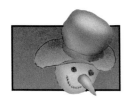

I go to a garden to ask the scarecrow:
"How can I learn to fly in the wind?"

"It must be easy, Simon," said the scarecrow.
"Even the birds know how to do it."

I go to the river to meet the birds.

My friend Marlene brings an airplane.
I talk to the birds and ask them:
"Will you pull us in the wind?"

But the birds are flying far away,
And don't know when they will return.

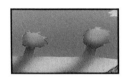

I lie on the grass and ask the sun:
"How can I learn to fly in the wind?"

"It must be easy, Simon," said the sun.
"Even the clouds know how to do it."

I ride up a mountain to talk to the clouds.

But the clouds turn to rain
And I must run home.

I go to a field to look for my friends.

I cannot fly in the wind like a bubble,
or like the birds
or like the clouds.

But I can make other things fly.

TO ARIANE

© 1989, Gilles Tibo
Published in Canada by Tundra Books, Montreal, Quebec H3G 1R4
Published in the United States by Tundra Books of Northern New York, Plattsburgh, NY 12901
Distributed in the United Kingdom by Ragged Bears Ltd., Andover, Hampshire SP11 9HX

ISBN 0-88776-234-4
Library of Congress Catalog Card Number   - 89-50777

Also available in a French edition, *Simon et le vent d'automne:*
ISBN 0-88776-235-2
Library of Congress Catalog Card Number   - 89-50776

Canadian Cataloguing in Publication Data: Tibo, Gilles, 1951– [Simon et le vent d'automne. English] Simon and the wind.

Translation of: Simon et le vent d'automne.   I. Title. II. Title: Simon et le vent d'automne. English.
ISBN 0-88776-234-4   PS8589.I26S5313 1989 jC843'.54 C89-090217-8 PZ7.T42Si 1989

The publisher has applied funds from its Canada Council block grant for 1989 toward the editing and production of this book.

Printed in Hong Kong by South China Printing Co. (1988) Ltd.